P9-DEG-467

I CAN BE ANYTHING!

BY JERRY SPINELLI   ILLUSTRATED BY JIMMY LIAO

LITTLE, BROWN AND COMPANY
Books for Young Readers
New York   Boston

Queen Anne's Co Free Library
Centreville, MD 21617

Copyright © 2010 by Jerry Spinelli
Illustrations copyright © 2010 by Jimmy Liao

All rights reserved. Except as permitted under the U.S. Copyright Act of 1976, no part of this publication may be reproduced, distributed, or transmitted in any form or by any means, or stored in a database or retrieval system, without the prior written permission of the publisher.

Little, Brown Books for Young Readers

Hachette Book Group
237 Park Avenue, New York, NY 10017
Visit our Web site at www.lb-kids.com

Little, Brown Books for Young Readers is a division of Hachette Book Group, Inc.
The Little, Brown name and logo are trademarks of Hachette Book Group, Inc.

First Edition: March 2010

Library of Congress Cataloging-in-Publication Data

Spinelli, Jerry.
  I can be anything! / Jerry Spinelli; illustrated by Jimmy Liao. — 1st ed.
     p. cm.
  Summary: A little boy ponders the many possible jobs in his future, from paper-plane folder and puppy-dog holder to mixing-bowl licker and tin-can kicker.
  ISBN 978-0-316-16226-5
  [1. Stories in rhyme.] I. Jimi, ill. II. Title.
  PZ8.3.S7592Iag 2010
  [E]—dc22   2008049177

10 9 8 7 6 5 4 3 2 1

TWP

Printed in Singapore

The illustrations for this book were done in watercolor and acrylic on watercolor paper. The text was set in ITC Clearface, and the display type is ITC Franklin Gothic.

When I grow up, what shall I be?

Of all the many, many jobs,

which one will be the best for me?

pumpkin grower

dandelion blower

puppy-dog holder

apple chomper

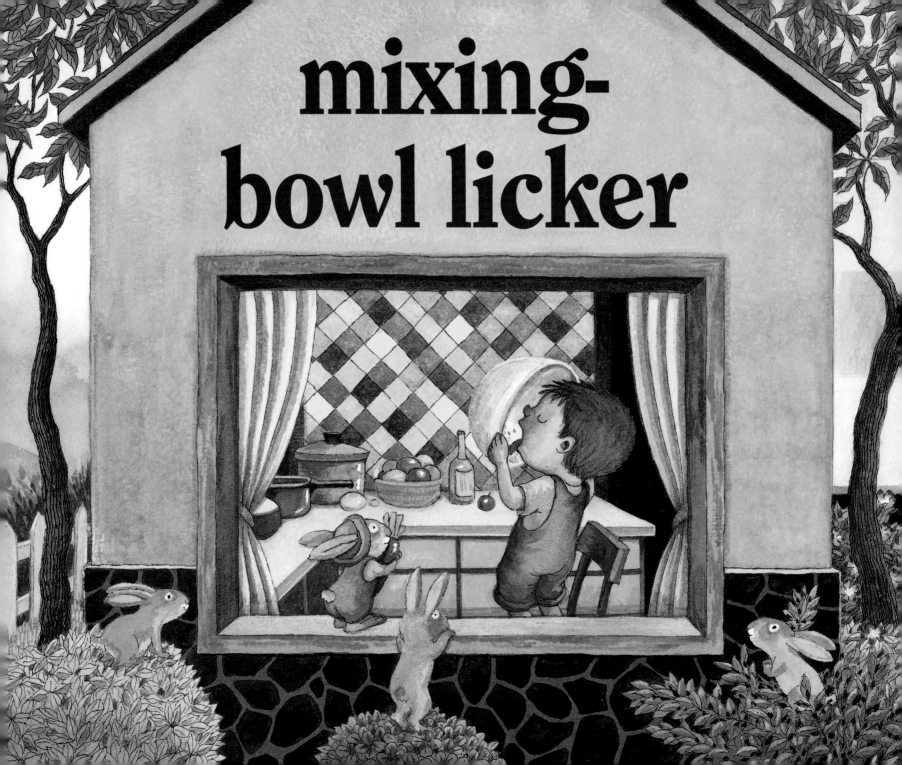

mixing-
bowl licker

tin-can kicker

barefooted hopper

bubble gum popper

snowball smoother

gift unwrapper

jump and clapper

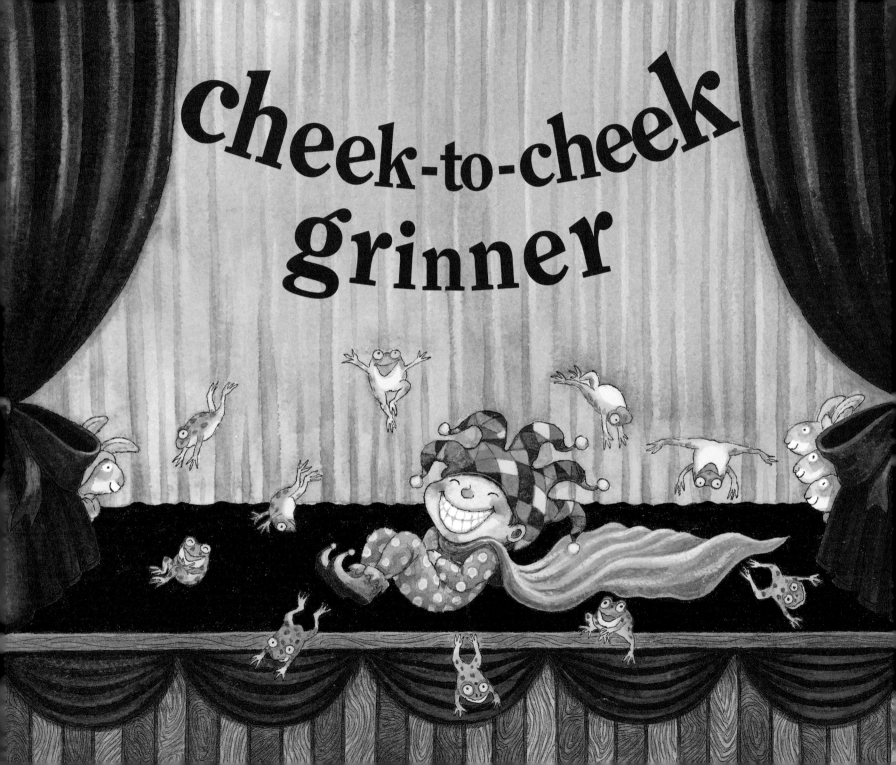

cheek-to-cheek
grinner

make-believe critter

deep-hole digger

lemonade swigger

silly-joke teller

best-part saver

EVERY

good-bye waver

So many jobs!

They're all such fun—

ONE!

I'm going to choose...

CEN c1